KV-383-509

© 2019 Disney/Pixar
Published by Hachette Partworks Ltd.
ISBN: 978-1-909766-71-6
Date of Printing: April 2019
Printed in Romania by Canale

**Disney·PIXAR**

**hachette**

Long ago in the Scottish Highlands, there was a kingdom called DunBroch, which was full of stories, magic… and danger.

DunBroch's king was Fergus. He had only one leg, the result of a fierce fight with Mor'du, a demon bear. Fergus and his queen, Elinor, had three mischievous sons and an older daughter, Merida.

Queen Elinor tried to teach Merida
how to be a dignified princess. But
Merida much preferred to spend her
time in the forest, riding her
beloved horse, Angus, and
practising archery.

One day, Queen Elinor announced
that there was to be a tournament.
"You will marry the winner," she
told her daughter.
"I won't do it!" cried Merida.

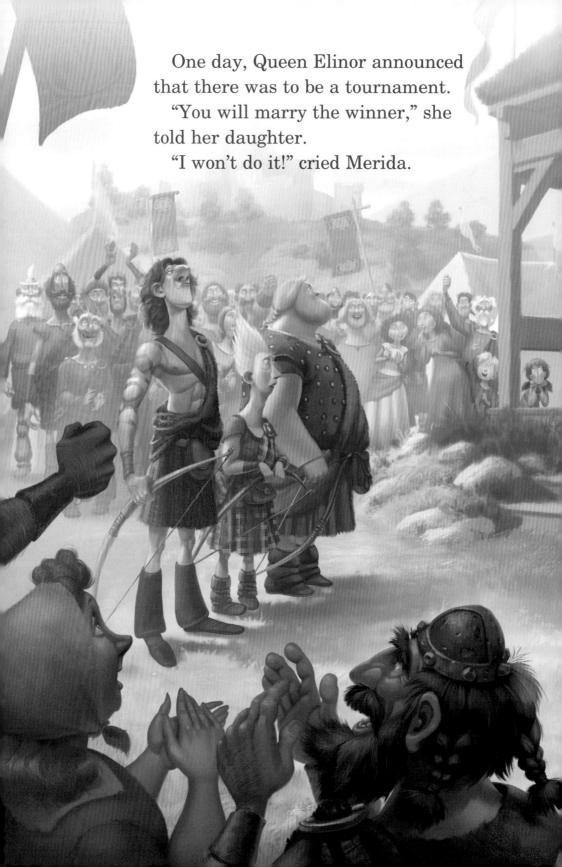

But a few days later, the lords MacGuffin,
MacIntosh and Dingwall presented their sons to the
King and Queen and the tournament began.

Queen Elinor asked Merida to choose the challenge.
"I choose archery," she said.

After the young men had taken their shots, Merida strode onto the field. "I'm shooting for my *own* hand!" she declared. Merida took aim and hit three bull's-eyes in a row!

Back at the palace, Merida and her mother had a terrible argument. Merida slashed a tapestry of the family, and Queen Elinor threw Merida's bow into the fire.

Merida rode Angus into the forest
and came upon some blue lights,
which guided her to a cottage – with
a witch in it! Merida asked for a spell
to change her mother so she would not force
Merida to marry. The Witch told Merida about a
prince who had asked for the strength of ten men.
"His destiny was changed forever," said the Witch.
"Then that's what I want," said Merida.
The Witch took an enchanted cake from her
cauldron and gave it to Merida.

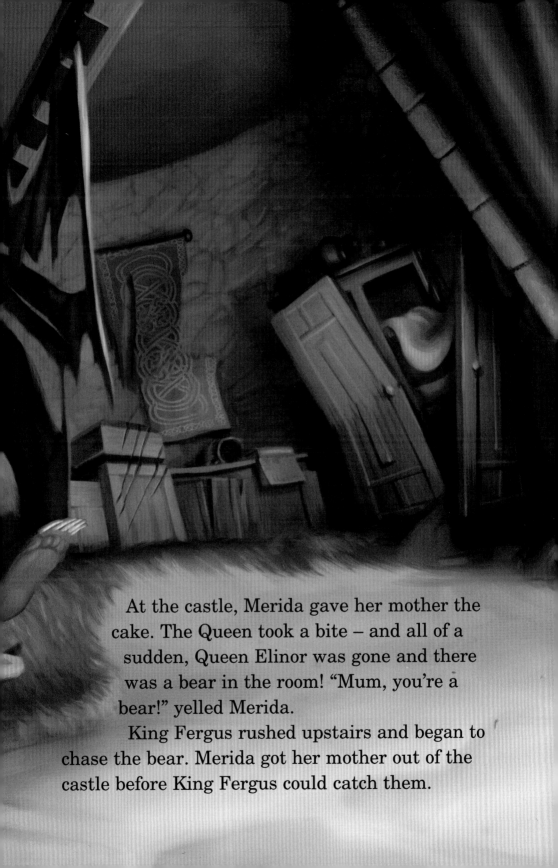

At the castle, Merida gave her mother the cake. The Queen took a bite – and all of a sudden, Queen Elinor was gone and there was a bear in the room! "Mum, you're a bear!" yelled Merida.

King Fergus rushed upstairs and began to chase the bear. Merida got her mother out of the castle before King Fergus could catch them.

Merida took her mother
back to the Witch's cottage, but
the old woman was gone. All she
had left behind was a note, saying: *'Fate be
changed, look inside; mend the bond torn by
pride.'* What could it mean?

The next morning, Merida taught her
mother how to fish. They had fun together!

For a moment, Queen Elinor's eyes turned
black and cold, just like a wild bear's. Then, just
as quickly, she turned back to normal. Merida
realised that her mother was becoming less and
less human – soon she would be 100% bear!

Another trail of lights led Merida and
Queen Elinor to an ancient castle, where
Merida spotted a stone tablet. It was
engraved with a picture of four princes,
but the fourth prince had broken off.
Merida noticed claw marks all around
the castle. At once, she understood the Witch's
tale about the prince: he had been turned into
Mor'du the bear – and this was his castle!
Mor'du appeared and attacked Merida, but
Elinor-Bear leapt to her daughter's defence.
Merida was saved.

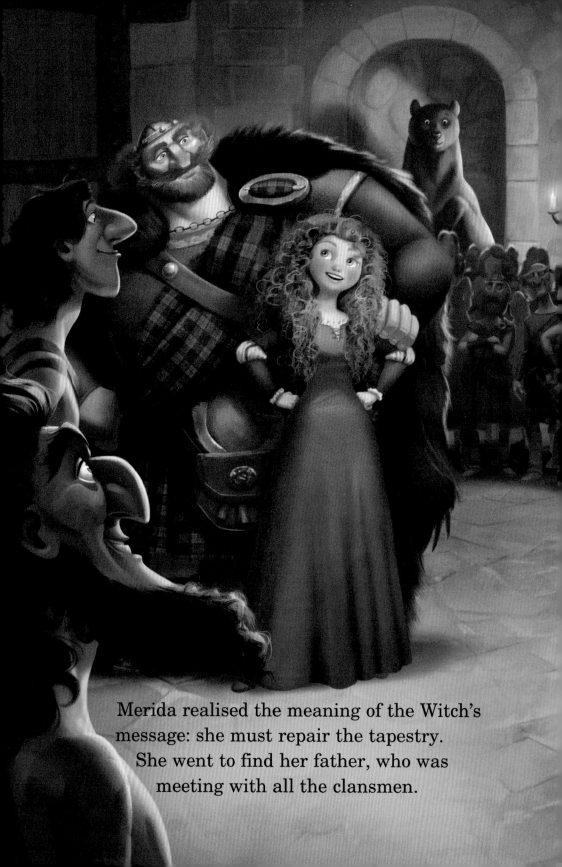

Merida realised the meaning of the Witch's
message: she must repair the tapestry.
She went to find her father, who was
meeting with all the clansmen.

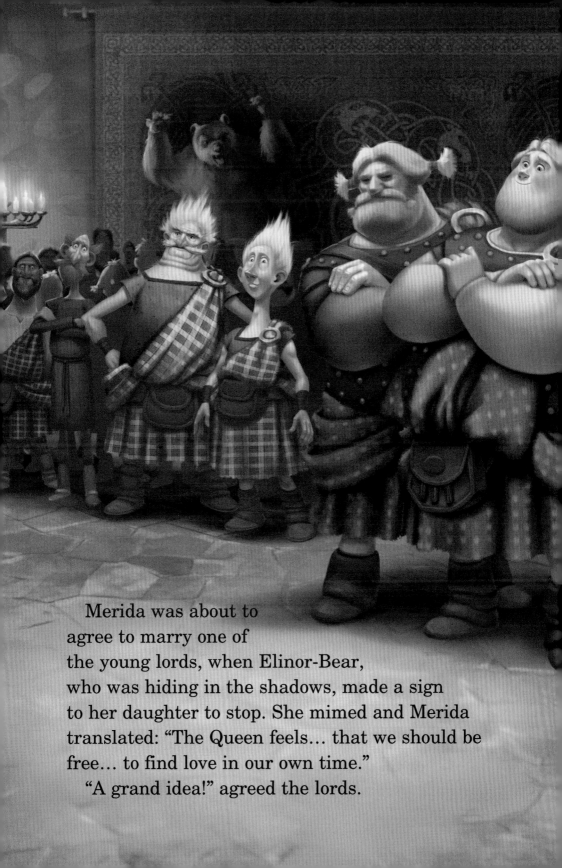

Merida was about to
agree to marry one of
the young lords, when Elinor-Bear,
who was hiding in the shadows, made a sign
to her daughter to stop. She mimed and Merida
translated: "The Queen feels... that we should be
free... to find love in our own time."
"A grand idea!" agreed the lords.

As Merida and Elinor-Bear sneaked to the tapestry room, King Fergus found them. He locked Merida up and set off after Elinor-Bear.

Just then, Merida spotted three bear cubs. Her brothers had eaten the enchanted cake and had turned into bears, too! The cubs let Merida out and they all galloped off on Angus. As they rode, Merida worked on the torn tapestry.

King Fergus and the lords
captured Elinor-Bear, but Merida
found them and began a sword fight
with her father.

Mor'du appeared and lunged at Merida.
Elinor-Bear broke free and charged Mor'du,
pushing him into a huge stone, which toppled
over and crushed him. In an instant, the ancient
prince's soul became a blue light and flew away.

Merida had mended the torn tapestry, so why hadn't her mother turned back into a human? Merida wanted Queen Elinor back the way she was. She no longer wanted to change her mother.

Dawn broke, and as the sun's rays touched Elinor-Bear, she changed back into a human! Then the bear cubs became boys again and everyone piled in for a big group hug. The family was together again!